LUCKY

THE PUPPY PLACE

Baxter

Bear

Buddy

Chewy and Chica

Cody

Flash

Goldie

Honey

Jack

Lucky

Maggie and Max

Noodle

Patches

Princess

Pugsley

Rascal

Scout

Shadow

Snowball

Sweetie

LUCKY

ELLEN MILES

SCHOLASTIC INC.

New York   Toronto   London   Auckland
Sydney   Mexico City   New Delhi   Hong Kong

ISBN 978-0-545-08347-8

Cover art by Tim O'Brien
Original cover design by Steve Scott

20 19   17 18 19/0

Printed in the U.S.A.   40

This edition first printing, February 2010

For Craig, with love and gratitude

CHAPTER ONE

"This isn't exactly the best weather for a camp-out." Charles's mother frowned as she looked up at the low, gray sky. She turned on the wind-shield wipers as she backed the van out of the driveway. "Are you sure you want to do this tonight?"

"Definitely." Charles didn't care one bit if it drizzled. He couldn't wait. He turned to look at his camping gear, which filled up the whole back-seat. Was everything there? He saw his sleeping bag, his brand-new tent, and the air mattress. Plus, he'd stuffed his pajamas, a flashlight, and a toothbrush into his backpack. Check. He was all set. "It'll be great practice for our Cub Scout campout this summer."

Charles faced front again, just as they drove past his best friend Sammy's house, next door. He felt a little twinge in his stomach. He had not told Sammy about the sleepover in his new friend David's backyard.

Charles didn't know David very well. Nobody did. David was in Charles and Sammy's class at school. He was a small, quiet boy with a small, quiet voice. His family had moved to town a few months ago, and he had still hardly said one word in class. Sometimes you could almost forget that he was there.

But this week things had started to change. The first thing that happened was at recess on Monday. Charles was playing left field in a kickball game when he noticed that some third graders were teasing David, over near the monkey bars.

David looked scared and upset, and Charles wasn't sure what to do. Mrs. P, the teacher on playground duty, was busy comforting a crying kindergartner over by the swings.

"Hey, David!" Charles called. "We need you on our team!" He pointed to right field, near the swings. Nobody ever kicked to right field, but it wasn't a bad idea to have somebody there just in case.

At first David looked surprised. But then he pushed past the third graders and ran over to take his position. Afterward, when Charles told him he'd done a great job, David just looked down at his shoes. He cleared his throat as if he were about to speak, but nothing came out.

On Tuesday, during free reading time, Charles waved David over to where he was sitting, in the corner near Huey the guinea pig's cage. They sat together and read, without talking. But just before the bell rang, Charles asked David about the book he was reading and David mumbled a few words. On Wednesday, Sammy was out sick and Charles saved Sammy's usual seat for David at lunch. It wasn't easy to get David talking, especially in the middle of the noisy cafeteria, but when Charles asked him about his favorite foods, they had a pretty good conversation. (Charles voted for pizza, David for grilled cheese sandwiches.)

Ever since then, David and Charles had talked a little bit every day. Charles had told David all about how his family liked to foster puppies. "That means that we take care of puppies who need a home, just until we can find them the perfect forever family." He told David about his older sister, Lizzie, and his younger brother, Adam (known as the Bean), and how they both loved puppies, too. And he told David all about Buddy, the best puppy ever, who had started out as a foster puppy but who had become a permanent part of the Peterson family.

David didn't have a dog, or any brothers and sisters. But little by little he told Charles about

4

how he and his parents liked to go hiking and biking together and about the camping trips they went on every summer. Last year they had gone to the Grand Canyon.

"I'm going camping for the first time this summer, with Cub Scouts," Charles told David. He knew it wasn't much compared to the Grand Canyon, but he was excited. "I got a tent for Christmas, so I'm all ready."

"Do you know how to set it up?" David asked.

"Well, not exactly." Actually, Charles didn't have a clue.

"Maybe if you bring it over, I could help you figure it out, since I've put up lots of tents." That was one of the longest sentences David had ever said.

And that's how the idea had started for this Friday-night campout in David's backyard. It was going to be great. David said his house had woods in back of it, and a stream, so it would be almost like camping in the wilderness. Charles couldn't wait. He didn't care that the ground would be soggy because it had been raining almost every day for the last two weeks. He wasn't worried about bugs or snakes. His new tent would keep them out. And he wasn't scared of the dark, because he had an excellent flashlight with brand-new batteries.

The only not-so-good thing was when he thought about Sammy. Charles knew that Sammy might feel bad when he found out that Charles had camped out with David. Sammy and Charles were in Cub Scouts together, and they had done a lot of planning for their very first campout. And now Charles was going on his very first campout. Without Sammy.

He had thought of asking David to invite Sammy, too, but something told him that would not be a good idea. David would talk to Charles now when they were alone, but he was still really, really quiet when he was in a group. And Sammy — well, Sammy wasn't shy at all. He was kind of the opposite. If you put Sammy in the same tent with David, one thing was for sure: David would clam up and Sammy would be doing all the talking. So far, Sammy didn't even seem to notice that Charles and David were making friends.

Charles tried to put all of that out of his mind once he got to David's house. The boys got busy right away at their campsite, out back beside the little stream — which was more like a little river now. All the rain they'd been having had made it much wider and deeper than usual. David's yard really was like the wilderness, with deep, thick woods on either side of the stream. And David really did know a lot about setting up tents. He showed Charles how to figure out which pole went where. It was still drizzling, but they didn't care. When they finally got the tent up, it looked perfect. They blew up their air mattresses and laid out their sleeping bags, then went inside for dinner.

David's mom had made meat loaf, one of Charles's favorites. He had three helpings, with lots of ketchup. To be polite, he also had a little bit of salad and a baked potato. Afterward, they had brownies with ice cream. Charles was stuffed. When he saw David's parents settle onto the big comfy couch in the TV room to watch a movie, Charles almost wished he and David were staying inside — but there was no way he was going to say that. Anyway, the tent was all ready for them.

They changed into their p.j.'s, brushed their teeth, and said good night to David's parents. Then Charles and David grabbed their flashlights and headed out into the damp, drizzly night.

Being in the tent was cool, like being outside and at the same time being all safe and cozy in your own little house. Once the boys were all zipped into their sleeping bags, they kept their flashlights on and talked for a while.

Charles told David a few of his favorite jokes, like "What do sea monsters eat? Fish and ships!"

David told Charles about some of the other places his family had gone camping, like in Wyoming and South Carolina. "Tomorrow I'll show you my collection of state park patches."

Finally, they turned off their flashlights and tried to go to sleep.

Charles lay there and listened to the patter of rain on the tent's roof. It was raw and chilly outside, but he was snug and warm inside his sleeping bag. At first the ground felt hard, even through his air mattress, and he thought he would never fall asleep. But he must have, because the next thing he heard was a loud rumble and a sudden bang, and he sat up straight, wide awake. Now the rain pounded overhead. The wind roared through the trees, and the tent rattled and shook.

Crack! Lightning lit up David's frightened face. He was wide awake, too. "Maybe we'd better —"

Charles began, but just then he heard David's dad shouting from outside the tent.

"Come on, boys!" He had to yell, to be heard over the wind and rain. "Time to call it a night and head inside."

Charles could already see water seeping in around the bottom of the tent. He and David grabbed their flashlights, unzipped the tent door, and crawled out.

"Some storm, huh?" David's father called over his shoulder as he led them toward the house.

When they got to the back door, Charles turned to take one last look at the tent. Was it going to blow completely away before he'd even spent one full night in it? He aimed his flashlight into the yard — and saw something he did not expect to see.

"Whoa." Charles shivered, and the hairs on the back of his neck stood up.

David turned to look, too. "What is that?" His voice was shaky.

Charles tried to hold his flashlight steady. He couldn't make out anything but two bright, glowing points of green. Eyes! They stared back at him shining in the dark. *Whose* eyes? Then there was a crack of thunder. A jagged bolt of lightning lit up the yard as bright as day — but just for a second. Afterward, Charles squinted into the dark. He couldn't believe what he had seen in that one bright moment. Then something moved in his flashlight beam, and the glowing eyes were gone.

"Come on, boys." David's father stood on the back porch, holding the door open.

"Wait!" Charles couldn't seem to move a muscle. "I think there's a puppy out there."

CHAPTER TWO

David's dad came over to look. He shined his flashlight all over the backyard. There was nothing to see but big, fat raindrops shining silvery in the beam of yellow light. "It was probably just a raccoon or something." He patted Charles on the shoulder. "What would a puppy be doing out in this crazy storm?"

Now David's mother was at the back door, lit up by the porch light. "You boys must be soaked. Come on in."

"But I have to —"

"You have to come in, that's what. You can't stay out there in that wild, windy night." David's mother shooed Charles inside.

Charles really wanted to go look for the puppy, but David's mother was not about to let him. Besides, she was right. He was soaked — and cold, too. So cold his teeth chattered. Charles followed David and his dad inside, where David's mom waited. "Get your wet things off, put these on, and hop right into bed." She handed a clean, dry pair of pajamas to each boy. "You'll warm up in no time."

Even though David didn't have a brother, he had bunk beds in his room. Charles thought that was the coolest thing. Every night, David could choose to sleep on either the top or the bottom bunk, depending on his mood.

Charles and David changed into the dry p.j.'s. David's pajamas were a little small on Charles, but he was happy to be out of his wet ones. David climbed up onto the top bunk and cleared off a bunch of action figures, tossing them onto the floor. "Okay, which bunk do you want?"

Charles was too tired to care. "You might as well stay up there." He yawned as he crawled into the bottom bunk.

"All set?" David's mom popped her head into the room. "Sleep well, boys. It's very late. You can camp out another night." She switched off the light.

Charles thought he would fall asleep right away, but he didn't. Instead, he just lay there and thought about what he had seen. He pictured the small, scruffy, gray-and-white face that had peered back at him through the raindrops when lightning lit up the yard. Raccoons weren't gray, were they?

Charles lay on his back, then on his right side, then on his left, then on his stomach. He felt wide awake. And worried. That poor, poor puppy, out there all alone in the rain. It must be a stray, a puppy that had run away from home and gotten lost in the storm. Maybe he should sneak out and look for it.

The wind slammed against the house, and a clap of thunder made the windows rattle. Rain pounded on the roof. Charles slid a little deeper under the covers.

Above him, he heard the springs of the upper bunk squeak as David turned over, then turned over again. "David?" Charles reached up to poke the bottom of the mattress. "Are you awake?"

David hung his head down over the edge of the bunk. Charles could just make out his face in the light that spilled in from the hallway. "Wide awake," David whispered. "I can't stop thinking about that — whatever it was."

"It was a puppy," Charles said. "I'm positive."

"I think so, too." David nodded, upside down.

"I want to go find him," Charles said.

"No way! My mom would have a fit." A flash of lightning from outside the window lit up David's worried face.

Charles knew his friend was right. And at that moment, he was almost glad that Sammy wasn't there. Sammy probably would have tried to talk them into searching for the puppy right then, storm or not. But Charles knew that was crazy. By now, the puppy could be anywhere. Hopefully it had found a safe place to hide from the raging storm. "But let's go out first thing in the morning, okay?"

"Deal." David's head disappeared from the edge of the bed, and a minute later Charles heard him sigh as the bed springs squeaked one more time. Then Charles turned over, too, and closed his eyes, and went to sleep.

When he woke up, the room was full of light. "Hey!" He kicked at the upper mattress. "It's morning. And the storm's over."

David swung his feet over the side and climbed down the ladder. "Let's go. Mom and Dad always sleep really late on Saturdays. I bet we'll find that puppy before they're even up."

They changed out of their p.j.'s and ran right downstairs and out the back door, without stopping for breakfast. The backyard was a squashy mess. Charles's tent was still up, but it was saggy and surrounded by puddles. The stream was muddy and brown and high on its banks, and the yard was full of fallen tree branches. But the sun was shining, and birds sang in the thick woods.

"Where do we start?" David looked up and down the stream.

Charles stood near the rain-soaked tent. "I think the puppy was right around here when I first saw his eyes glowing back at me." He pointed to a spot nearby. "Maybe he was curious about the tent."

"I hope he stayed on this side of the stream." David glanced nervously at the rushing water. "I'm not supposed to go near it when the water's running this high. If Dad says it's too dangerous for me, think about a little puppy. See, usually there are stepping-stones right there." David pointed to a narrow part of the stream. "But they've been underwater since it started raining."

"It's kind of cool when the water's so high." Maybe the water was dangerous, but Charles liked to watch it splash and roll.

"This is nothing." David tossed in a stick and they watched it zoom away, carried by the strong current. "You should have seen it last week." He started off up the stream.

Charles followed David. They splooshed along the muddy path that ran next to the stream, scanning the woods on both sides for any sign of a puppy. Soon Charles's sneakers were covered in goopy, gluey mud, but he barely noticed. He was too busy looking for puppy tracks. "Nothing," he muttered to himself. He was disappointed. "The rain must have washed everything away."

"Hey!" David had run ahead. Now he was standing near a big boulder. He waved to Charles.

"Check it out." Charles ran to catch up. David pointed to where a big log lay across the path. Beneath it was a little cavelike space, protected from the rain. And there, in the older, harder mud, was an animal track.

Charles bent to look. Yes! It looked just like one of Buddy's footprints, a pad and four little toes. He noticed a blotch between two of the toes, a rusty brown stain on the lighter-colored dry mud. "That's no raccoon." Charles felt his heart start to pound. "That's definitely a puppy track. And it looks like the puppy might be hurt. I think that's blood!" He picked up a stick and poked a little at the track. "Definitely. It's blood, all right."

"*Shh!*" David grabbed his shoulder. "Look!"

Charles turned and saw a little face staring back at him from behind a bush. Two brown eyes, opened wide in fear, peered through a mop of gray-and-white fur. The puppy! He was about Buddy's size, probably no more than six months old, and so skinny that his ribs showed. He didn't look like any of the dogs on Lizzie's "Dog Breeds of the World" poster, so he must be a mix. He held up one paw, and Charles saw red. Blood. So he was right: The puppy was hurt. The little dog didn't move; he seemed frozen in place.

I'm lost and all alone. I need help — but I'm scared.

When Charles took a step toward him, the puppy disappeared in a flash of gray and white. Even though he was limping, he moved quickly through the trees, up the stream and away from the boys.

Charles stumbled and nearly fell as he and David raced over roots and rocks, trying to catch up. But it was no use. The puppy was gone without a trace.

CHAPTER THREE

"Now what?" David peered into the thick, jungly woods.

Charles pictured the puppy's face. The poor thing. He was obviously frightened. He was way too skinny, and his mud-covered fur was matted and tangled. He had been on his own for more than a day or two. And if the puppy had ever worn a collar, it must have fallen off.

Now Charles pictured Buddy, curled up nose to tail with his ears hanging off the foot of Charles's bed, where he loved to snooze. Buddy's brown-and-white coat was always clean and soft and smooth, and his round puppy belly was always full of delicious food. But Buddy was safe at home, and this puppy was out in the world on his own. What if Buddy ran away and got lost? After a few days he would probably look and act a lot like the gray-and-white puppy. Somebody probably loved this puppy just as much as Charles loved Buddy.

"We have to help him." Charles swallowed hard so he wouldn't cry.

David nodded. "Sure. But first we have to find him."

"Okay." Charles spun around in a circle. Then he stopped and pointed into the woods. "You go that way, the way he ran. I'll go back the way we came. Maybe he'll circle around to where we first saw him." He knew he sounded bossy, but he didn't care. They had to find that puppy.

"O-kay." David spoke slowly. "But —"

Charles was already heading back along the stream. "Just yell if you see him," he called back over his shoulder. Charles scanned the woods as he walked, watching for a flash of gray or white. The mud sucked at his sneakers, and bugs flew around his face. One buzzed right into his ear, and Charles shook his head angrily. "Where is that puppy?" His voice was loud in the silent woods.

Something rustled in the bushes. Charles stopped and stood as still as he could. He held his breath. He looked from side to side, moving only his eyes.

A small brown bird hopped out of a thorny shrub and cocked its head at Charles as if to say, "What are you doing in my woods?"

Charles sighed and began to walk again, looking down at his feet now and then to watch for tracks. All he could see were his own sneaker prints, all mixed up with David's. Not a puppy print in sight.

"Charles! Charles!" David called in a loud, hoarse whisper. Charles looked up just in time to see the shaggy gray-and-white puppy picking his way through the woods, moving toward Charles and the stream. David followed the puppy, pushing through the prickly branches and hanging vines.

Charles took three running steps and dove for the puppy. The puppy picked up speed and veered away at the last minute, like a quarterback on his way to the end zone. Charles landed face-first and empty-handed in the soft, sticky mud. *"Oof."*

The puppy didn't even slow down.

Phew. I got away! I better keep running, and running, and running.

Charles looked up just in time to see the puppy dash madly through David's backyard. It made a wide circle, then ran back up the stream.

"He sure is fast when he wants to be." David caught up with Charles. "He popped out of the woods, took one look at me, and ran off like a rabbit."

Charles stood up and wiped some mud off his nose. "I guess we just have to run faster next time."

"I don't know — I think when we chase him, we just scare him even more," David said. "He's really frightened. And did you see how skinny he is?"

Charles remembered the way the puppy's ribs had stuck out. David was right. The little dog was skinny and scared and hurt. "Lizzie says you should be really careful around frightened dogs, because they'll sometimes bite just out of fear." Lizzie knew a lot about dogs.

David shook his head. "Not this puppy. He won't bite. I looked right into his eyes. He isn't the biting type."

For once, David didn't sound shy. He sounded sure of himself and Charles believed him. He nodded. "So, what do we do next? We need a plan."

"Okay." David rubbed his stomach. "But —
aren't you starving? I am. I'm so hungry I can't
even think anymore."

The boys made their way back down the stream
and headed toward the house, keeping an eye out
for the puppy. At the back door, David looked at
Charles. "Um —"

Charles looked down at his muddy front. What
a mess. He knew his mom would kill him if he
went into his own house dripping with mud.
David's parents probably wouldn't be too happy,
either. "Maybe I better not come in."

David nodded. "I'll be right back." He kicked off
his sneakers and slipped inside. A few minutes
later he came back with an armload of food: two
leftover baked potatoes, a couple of juice boxes, a
brownie, and a foil-covered plate. He handed
Charles a juice box and a potato. They sat down
cross-legged on the deck and ate quickly, wash-
ing down the dry potatoes with juice and splitting
the brownie for dessert.

Still hungry, Charles looked at the plate. "What's that?"

"This," said David, "is our puppy bait." He pulled away the foil to reveal two thick slices of meat loaf. "That hungry puppy won't be able to resist this."

CHAPTER FOUR

"Great idea." Charles was impressed with David's plan. Why hadn't he thought of that?

"It was obvious as soon as I saw the meat loaf in the fridge." David shrugged, as if it were nothing. "I figured, if the puppy is that hungry, maybe we can tempt him to come to us."

Charles nodded as he took a slice of meat loaf off the plate. He couldn't stop himself from taking just a little nibble of it. Even cold, it was better than leftover baked potatoes. Charles knew Buddy would be drooling if he smelled something that yummy. "So now what?"

David had a plan. "Maybe we should go back up the stream to that log where we saw the paw

28

print. He's been near that spot at least twice. He might circle back to it again. If we quit chasing him, maybe we can lure him over to us." He stopped talking and blushed, looking down at his feet.

"Another great idea." Charles gave David a little punch in the arm, and David blushed some more. David didn't seem nearly as shy as before. Maybe he was getting used to being around Charles. And he sure was full of ideas. In fact, Charles thought, maybe David and Sammy weren't so different after all. They were both idea people.

The boys splooshed up the muddy path again and headed for the fallen log near the boulder. "Right here?" Charles pointed to the log.

"*Shhh!*" David turned to face him with his finger up to his lips. "We don't want to scare him off." David set a chunk of meat loaf on a flat rock in the middle of the path. Then he sat down on

the muddy ground near the log and folded himself up so small that he was almost hidden
behind the big rock. Charles hunkered down next
to him. They sat in silence for a few minutes and
scanned the woods.

A mosquito started to buzz around Charles's
ears. Why did bugs always *bug* you when you
sat still? He shook his head, but it didn't go
away. Finally, he had to reach up and swat it.
Dratted bugs, as Dad would say. "So, what if the
puppy comes?" He knew he was supposed to be
quiet but he couldn't help himself. "Should I try
to grab him?"

David shook his head hard. "No. He's scared.
We have to be really gentle with him, and stay
down at his level. We probably look like giants
to him."

Charles stared at him. "Where did you learn
so much about dogs, when you don't even
have one?"

"I guess I'm good with animals." David shrugged. "That's what my mom says, anyway." Then he seemed to remember about being quiet. He stopped and put his finger over his lips.

They waited.

And waited.

Charles started to get a cramp in his leg. But just as he was about to straighten it, David put a hand on his arm. "There he is." David pointed. "See him?"

Sure enough, the gray-and-white puppy limped out of the brush, his nose in the air as he sniffed his way toward the meat loaf. Charles could tell that he did not see the two boys hiding near the food.

Slowly but steadily, glancing from side to side, the puppy headed for the tasty treat.

I am so, so hungry. This could be dangerous, but I have to risk it.

With one quick movement, the puppy grabbed the meat loaf in his mouth and backed away to gobble it down.

Next to Charles, David moved one arm v-e-r-y s-l-o-w-l-y and tossed another chunk of meat loaf onto the rock.

The puppy ran a few steps away, looking over his shoulder in fear. Then he turned, sat down, and watched for a moment. Charles saw him sniff and sniff again at the air, then lick his lips. The boys stayed as still as they could. Finally, the puppy took one step closer, then another, then three more darting steps toward the food. He grabbed it and swallowed it down without backing away.

David tossed out another chunk. The puppy ate it. "Okay, good." David's voice was ten times quieter than usual. "That's good. Want some more?"

The puppy licked his lips.

I do *want some more. I could eat and eat and eat. Maybe I can trust this person.*

David tossed another piece of meat loaf. And another. He whispered gentle, encouraging words. Each time, the puppy took the food a little more quickly, a little more confidently.

Charles knew you had to be very gentle with shy puppies, but he wasn't nearly as patient as David. "Shouldn't I try to grab him?"

"Wait." David inched himself forward, toward the puppy. Slowly, he held out a chunk of meat loaf. Even more slowly, the puppy stepped forward and stretched out his neck to sniff. Then he snatched the treat and gulped it down. "Good dog," David murmured as he fed the puppy more pieces. "What a good dog." When he had gulped down the last little bit, the puppy turned to go.

Charles couldn't stand to let him get away. He

crawled quickly toward the puppy. "Here, boy," he said, as softly as he could.

The puppy's ears went back and he tucked his tail between his legs.

Alert! Alert! This new person is scary.

The puppy gave Charles a frightened look and dashed away, into the thick, deep woods.

CHAPTER FIVE

"Oh, man." Charles watched the last glimpse of gray disappear into the underbrush. He turned to David. "Sorry!"

"I almost had him." David glared at Charles. "Just a few more seconds and I think he would have let me touch him." His voice was shaky.

"I thought he was about to run away." Charles got up and dusted off his hands. "I'm really sorry."

"He was getting used to me." David plopped himself down on the log. "That puppy likes people, I'm sure of it. He wants to be friends. He's just scared." He was quiet for a moment. Then he sighed. "You know what? I'm still starving. Let's go get something to eat and figure out what to do next."

Charles and David headed back to the house. This time, Charles brushed the dried mud off his front, took off his shoes, and came inside.

David's parents sat at the kitchen table, drinking coffee and reading the paper. They were still in their pajamas. "Well, good morning." David's mother looked up when they came in. "I thought you boys were still asleep upstairs." She stretched and yawned. "How about some pancakes?"

Charles felt his stomach rumble. That baked potato had not filled him up one bit.

"Mom — Dad —" David began.

"Too bad about your campout last night." David's dad cleared newspapers away to make space at the table. "You guys almost got washed downstream."

Charles had almost forgotten about that. The wild, stormy night seemed far in the past. Right now, the only thing on his mind was that poor, scared stray puppy.

David seemed to feel the same way. "Dad —" he began again, more urgently. "The puppy! We saw him."

David's dad raised his eyebrows. "Are you sure?"

"Positive." David nodded.

"Puppy? What puppy?" David's mom seemed surprised.

David's dad turned to her. "The boys thought they saw a puppy last night."

"We did see a puppy. And he's out there now. He's really scared and shy, but we almost got him to trust us." David blurted it out.

David's mom put down her newspaper. "Trust you? What do you mean?" Suddenly, her face was serious.

That's when the whole story came out: the skinny stray puppy, the bloody paw prints, the meat loaf, all of it.

"Promise me you'll never feed a strange dog again." David's mom reached out to put a hand on his chin. She tilted it up and looked straight into his eyes. "I mean it. I know you have a way with animals, but still — you can never be sure."

"But the puppy!" David burst out. "We're not the ones in danger. What about the poor puppy?"

Charles figured it was time to speak up. "He really needs help."

David's dad nodded. "You're right. But maybe you boys could use some help, too." He put down his coffee cup. "Let's go find that puppy."

David's mom had to leave. "I have yoga class, but let me make you some breakfast first. You need your energy." She went right to the stove.

By the time the boys had finished the last forkfuls of the pancakes she'd made, David's dad was dressed and ready to go. They went outside and started to walk up the muddy trail beside the stream.

"Where did you see him last?" David's dad was all business. Charles and David showed him where the puppy had run out of the woods. Then they led him up the path to the boulder and pointed out the little paw prints underneath the log.

David's dad squatted down for a closer look. He nodded. "Those sure don't look like raccoon tracks." He stood up and looked around. "I don't know if he'll come to us again. He seems to keep heading upstream, so let's follow this path and watch for him. But I think David's right — we shouldn't chase him if we spot him. Just be still, be patient, and see what happens."

The three of them walked up the path, scanning the trail and the woods for any sign of the puppy.

Charles tried hard to walk very, very quietly. He put each foot down carefully, avoiding any sticks on the trail that might snap under his weight. Lizzie had told him that was how Native

Americans used to walk through the deep, dark forests. He walked so slowly that David's dad got pretty far ahead, but Charles hardly noticed.

"What's that sound?" Up ahead, David stood very still with his hand to his ear. "Do you hear that?"

"What?" Charles couldn't hear a thing but birds singing — and a mosquito buzzing in his ear. He brushed the mosquito away and listened harder. Then he heard it, too. A high-pitched, whimpering cry. It was very faint, but he heard it. "It's the puppy. Where is he?" Charles looked around wildly. But there was nothing to see. No tracks, no flash of gray and white. Nothing.

"Charles! Quick! Come here." David had run over to a cluster of pine trees. "Look." Charles helped him push aside a big, prickly branch.

Underneath the branches it was dark and cool and quiet. At first Charles couldn't see anything.

Then he spotted the puppy, curled up nose to tail in a little hollow it had scraped out of the dirt. "Oh!" Charles put his hand over his mouth. The puppy lay completely still, like an old, limp gray rag.

CHAPTER SIX

"Is he . . . ?" Charles swallowed back the word "dead." He couldn't stand to even say it out loud.

"I don't think so." David shook his head. "Maybe he's just really, really tired. And it looks like he threw up all that food we gave him."

"Ew." Charles felt his stomach flip when he saw the pile of barf near the puppy.

Just then, David's dad showed up. He pulled aside another branch so he could see, too. "Whoa." He let out a long, low whistle. "That's one sick pup."

The puppy opened one eye and stared up at them. Then he rolled onto his back and held up his injured foot. The blood was dry and brown now, instead of red, but you could tell that paw really hurt.

Help me. Please, please help me!

"We have to get him out of here." David's dad pulled off his sweatshirt. "We can carry him on this." Gently, he laid the sweatshirt down on the dirt, next to the puppy. Then he reached over and rolled the whimpering dog onto the shirt. "Okay, little guy," he murmured. "It's okay. We're here to help."

Charles could see where David got it from, that thing about being good with animals.

The boys got on their hands and knees and helped slide the sweatshirt, with the puppy on it, out from under the branches.

"Great." Slowly, David's dad stood up. "Now, let's lift him carefully and walk slowly back down the path. Okay?"

They made a good team. The puppy hardly weighed a thing. His eyes were open but he did not try to move, and he had stopped whimpering. Charles wasn't sure whether that was a good sign or a bad sign.

Back inside the house, they laid the puppy carefully on the living room rug. "He's cute," said David's father. "He reminds me of Buster, this mutt I had when I was a kid. My mom called him the 57 Variety Dog because he was a mix of so many different breeds."

Charles reached out very slowly and stroked the dog's dirty, matted fur. "We should take him to the vet. Dr. Gibson will know what to do."

"Right." David's dad nodded. "There's only one problem. No car. David's mom took it."

"What about your other car?" Charles asked.

"Our other car is my bike." David's dad gave Charles a crooked smile. "I ride it everywhere: to work, to the store, to the park. A family of three doesn't need two cars."

44

"We sure do today." David looked down sadly at the puppy.

"I'll call my parents." Charles knew they would help if they could. David brought him the phone, and Charles dialed. His dad picked up after three rings. "Dad! There's a puppy that needs our help."

Maybe it was because he was a firefighter, but Charles's dad was always ready to help. He drove right over.

Soon, David and Charles and their dads stood in a circle around the vet's tall metal table. The puppy lay still as Dr. Gibson, in her white coat, touched him all over, feeling for broken bones or other problems. She was completely silent as she focused on her job.

Charles held his breath. What would Dr. Gibson say?

Finally, after she had listened to the puppy's heart and lungs, the vet put down her stethoscope and looked around at everyone. She rested one hand gently on the puppy's side. "This is a very sick puppy." Her face was serious. "He's completely exhausted and nearly starving, and filthy and full of fleas and ticks, and he has a big cut on one paw, which has become infected. He has a high fever and he is badly dehydrated, which means his body needs lots and lots of fluids, mixed with medicine to stop the infection."

"Wow." Charles looked down at the limp gray puppy. "Can — can you help him?"

"I'll do my best." Dr. Gibson was still resting a hand on the puppy. "He'll have to stay overnight. Are you his owners?" She frowned at David's father.

"Oh — no, no, no." He held up his hands.

"He's a stray," Charles jumped in to explain. "He's not wearing a collar. I think he's been on his own for a while. He just showed up, in the woods behind David's house."

Dr. Gibson turned to David. "You've never seen him before, around the neighborhood?"

David couldn't seem to say a word. He blushed and shook his head.

"I don't think he belongs to any of the families nearby." David's dad put a hand on David's shoulder.

"Well, then." Dr. Gibson crossed her arms. "He'll still need a lot of care after I'm done with him. Can you handle that?"

David and his father looked at each other. "What about —" David began.

"I don't think that will work for us —" said David's father at the same time.

"We'll take him." Charles's dad interrupted both of them.

Charles stared at his dad. "Really? Shouldn't we ask Mom?"

Dad glanced at the limp, exhausted little pup. "I'm sure she'll agree that this puppy needs our help."

The puppy tried to sit up, but he was too weak. He settled back with a sigh.

These people are talking about me, I know. I think they'll help me.

Dr. Gibson stroked the puppy and nodded. "Good. I'll call you in the morning. You can see him tomorrow. Hopefully he'll make it through the night."

"What?" David stared at her.

Charles stared at the vet, too. *"Hopefully he'll make it?"* he asked. A bad taste came into his mouth. Was he going to throw up? He clenched his fists so hard that his fingernails dug into his palms. "What do you mean, hopefully he'll make it?"

Dr. Gibson's face softened. "He's a very sick puppy." Her voice was gentler now. "I promise to do every single thing I can to make him well. But — I can't promise that it will work."

CHAPTER SEVEN

That night, for the second night in a row, Charles could not get to sleep. He was so worried about the little stray puppy he could hardly stand it. He wished he could be at Dr. Gibson's office, lying on a cot next to the cage where the puppy would be spending the night. At least then there would be a reason for lying there awake. At least then he would be keeping the puppy company.

As it was, he lay still in the middle of his bed and stared at the glow-in-the-dark stars on his ceiling and thought over and over, *Please make it! Please get better, little puppy.* He pictured the puppy's sad brown eyes, and the way he had looked at him so pleadingly when they left him at the vet. Now and then Charles reached down to pet Buddy, who lay snoring softly at the end of the bed. Buddy would wake up just enough to lick his hand, which made Charles feel a tiny bit better.

As soon as it got light outside, Charles jumped out of bed and went downstairs. Buddy trotted behind him. The house was completely quiet, but when Charles got to the kitchen he saw that his dad was already up. He sat at the kitchen table with his hands cupped around a mug of coffee. He had dark circles under his eyes. "Hi, pal." He looked up when Charles walked in. "Sleep well?"

Charles shook his head.

"I didn't, either." His dad frowned down into his mug.

"I just kept thinking about the puppy's face." Charles let Buddy out the back door for a pee. He rubbed his eyes and yawned. "And the way he looked when we left him with Dr. Gibson."

"So did I." His dad got up to get another cup of coffee.

"Do you think he made it through the night?" Charles almost hated to ask. He let Buddy back in again and poured him a bowl of kibble.

"I'm sure Dr. Gibson will call soon." That was not really an answer to his question, but Charles didn't ask again. He just sat down next to his dad and leaned against him.

They sat quietly that way for a while. Finally, Charles had to say something. "Can we call *her*?"

His dad shook his head. "She's probably not at her office yet." He stroked Charles's hair. "Be patient."

When Buddy was done eating, Charles picked him up and held him on his lap. He patted Buddy's soft fur for a while. Then he put his head down on the table, resting it on his folded arms. He was so tired. Suddenly the phone rang, and he shot straight up in his seat. Buddy jumped off his lap. Charles's dad ran to answer the phone.

"Hello? Yes, Dr. Gibson?" Dad's voice was very serious. He listened for a moment. Then he smiled, and Charles let out the breath he had been holding. "Oh, that's terrific. Great news. Thanks. Yes, we'll be there. Thanks, Doc." He hung up and turned to Charles.

"He made it!" they yelled together. His dad came over to give Charles a hug and a high five. "He's much better already and we can pick him up later this morning. Isn't that great?"

"What happened?" Lizzie rubbed her eyes as she shuffled into the kitchen. "Is the puppy okay?" Charles and his dad had told the rest of the family the whole story at dinner the night before. Lizzie was worried about the puppy, too, of course — and worried about how upset his owners must be. She had already checked with the police and the animal shelter to make sure nobody had reported a stray puppy, and she'd started to make up some FOUND: LOST PUPPY signs to post around town.

"Yes! He's fine. He's great. He made it!" Charles pumped a fist in the air. He felt so happy.

"You should call David." Lizzie handed Charles the phone. "I'm sure the puppy whisperer is wondering, too."

Lizzie had told Charles about "horse whisperers," people who could tame wild horses just by talking softly into their ears. She kept calling David "the puppy whisperer," which made Charles a little bit jealous, until Lizzie said that Charles was kind of a puppy whisperer, too. "You're great with all the puppies we foster."

Charles dialed David's number and David picked up right away. He probably hadn't slept, either. While Charles told David about Dr. Gibson's call, Mom and the Bean came downstairs and Dad and Lizzie filled them in on the good news.

"David said we should stop by after we pick up the puppy." Charles hung up and turned to his dad. "His mom put my sleeping bag and tent out to dry, and we can pick them up. Plus, he can't wait to see the puppy." By then, the Bean was twirling and jumping all around the kitchen and Mom had started stirring up a batch of waffles, "to celebrate."

"This puppy is lucky to have made it." Dr. Gibson spoke very seriously when she brought the puppy out of his cage later that morning. "I sewed up the cut on his paw and wrapped up that foot so it can heal." She showed Charles and his dad how she had wrapped the sore foot in a sticky purple tape called vet wrap. "I gave him a lot of medicine and a lot of fluids, and some food — not too much at once, since that could make him sicker — and I've treated him for the fleas and ticks and made sure he's up to date on his shots so you don't have to worry about him being near Buddy."

Dr. Gibson patted the puppy gently. "He's basically a healthy dog, so he really perked up quickly. All he needs now is some more rest, a bath, and a lot of love. That last part shouldn't be hard. He's a real sweetheart. And such a cutie. I'd guess he's part schnauzer, maybe also part spaniel or poodle."

The puppy gazed up at her with his big brown eyes. Charles thought he looked much better. His fur was still matted and filthy, but he held his head high and wagged his tail when Dr. Gibson petted him. Dr. Gibson sighed and bent down to give him a kiss. "See what I mean? He's irresistible. And now that he knows he's safe, he's much less shy."

She helped Charles and his dad settle the puppy into a metal crate lined with soft old towels. They had brought it along so that he could ride comfortably and safely in the back of the van.

"What do we owe you?" Charles's dad reached for his wallet.

But Dr. Gibson shook her head. "We'll work

something out later. I'm always glad to help with the puppies you foster. Let me know how he does."

"We will." Charles got into the van, then rolled down the window. "And please let us know if you hear about some people looking for their puppy." He had already scanned all the signs on the clinic bulletin board, but there weren't any about a lost puppy.

When they pulled into David's driveway, Charles spotted David in the backyard, throwing sticks into the stream. David's mom greeted them and handed Charles the backpack he'd left in David's room. Then, while she and Charles's dad went to gather the rest of the camping equipment, Charles got out and went to the back of the van to check on the puppy. "Hi there, little guy." The puppy looked so much better. Charles opened the door of the crate so he could take him out and show him to David. He could hardly wait to hold him for the very first time.

But the puppy squirmed past Charles and jumped out of the van. "Hey!" Charles couldn't believe it. He watched in shock as the puppy limped quickly across the yard and began to head straight upstream, the same way he had gone all the other times. "Catch him!" Charles yelled, when he saw that David still had a chance to grab the puppy.

David knelt down as the puppy came toward him. He held out his hand and spoke softly, but the puppy just trotted along, despite his sore foot. In about three seconds, the puppy would be out of David's reach.

Charles couldn't help himself. "Cut out the puppy-whispering and *grab* him already," he yelled.

David looked up, surprised and hurt. And the puppy picked up speed as it trotted past him.

CHAPTER EIGHT

"Oh, no." Charles groaned and put his hands over his eyes. He couldn't stand to watch the puppy run away again, before he'd even had a chance to hold him. Charles knew it wasn't nice to yell at David that way, but come on! This was a time for action.

"Hold on there, you little squirt!" Charles heard David yell. He peeked between his fingers just in time to see David turn and make a diving tackle. A second later, David stood up — with the puppy in his arms. He walked toward Charles and the van.

"Nice." Charles had to admit that David had gotten the job done.

58

David didn't smile or meet Charles's eyes. "Right." He held the puppy close. "He's shaking."

The puppy struggled in David's arms, trying to get down.

Charles felt bad. The poor puppy had been through so much, and now this. But they couldn't let him run away. "Want me to take him?"

"Whatever." David let Charles take the puppy from his arms.

Charles could tell David was upset, but he couldn't think about that right now. He held the puppy close. He was light as a feather, compared to solid Buddy. His coat was rough, totally unlike Buddy's soft fur. And David was right: The puppy was shaking all over. He was panting, too. Lizzie said that sometimes meant that a dog was stressed out. "Poor thing." Charles nuzzled the puppy's neck, trying to calm him down. "It's okay, little guy. It's okay. We just didn't want you to run off again." The puppy seemed to relax as Charles murmured to it. Charles let out a long breath and looked up at David. "Sorry I yelled."

David shrugged. He wouldn't look at Charles.

"Really." Charles didn't know what else to say. Had he messed everything up? David was acting all shy again. "I'm sorry." Holding the puppy in one arm, he reached into his backpack and fumbled around. Ah! There it was. He pulled out a Snickers bar and held it out to David as a peace offering.

David hesitated. Then he took the candy bar, peeled open the wrapper, broke the bar in two, and handed half to Charles. They chewed silently for a few moments. Charles petted the puppy, and the puppy gave Charles's hand a little lick. He seemed to be settling down. He was a real cutie, even with that filthy, smelly, matted fur.

"Want to come over?" Charles asked. "Dr. Gibson said we should try giving him a bath today. We just have to put a plastic bag over his foot to keep the bandage dry." He looked David in the eye. "I could really use your help."

David nodded. "Okay."

"Where is everybody?" Charles thought the house seemed strangely quiet when he and his dad and David got back home. They had carried in the puppy's crate and set it down in a corner of the kitchen.

"Lizzie took Buddy over to play with Aunt Amanda's dogs." Dad looked at a note on the table. "She says here that she figured it might be best to have Buddy out of the house when the puppy first arrives."

The puppy was sort of squinched into one corner of his crate. He looked around with frightened eyes.

David knelt down and started talking softly to the puppy.

"What about Mom and the Bean?" Charles asked.

"The Bean is at a birthday party." Now Dad was staring into the fridge. Charles could tell he was thinking about lunch. "And Mom's at the office." That meant the office of the *Littleton News*, where Mom was a reporter. Mostly Mom worked at home, but if she was on a deadline she liked to work at the office on Sundays, when it was quiet there.

"Maybe we should let the puppy out so he can explore." The puppy had already started to look much more relaxed. It was just like Dr. Gibson had said: The puppy wasn't so shy now that he understood that he was safe and among friends.

"Why not? Maybe you and David can even give him that bath." Dad pulled some cheese and mustard out of the fridge and started making sandwiches.

Bang! The back door flew open with a crash, and Sammy bounced in. "Hey, everybody. What's for lunch?"

Charles and his father looked at each other and shook their heads. "You have a way of showing up at mealtimes, don't you, Sammy?" Charles's dad smiled as he took out two more pieces of bread.

"Whoa, who's this?" Sammy knelt down next to David to take a look at the puppy. "Hi, David. Hey, nice catch at kickball the other day. What are you doing here?"

David didn't answer. Shy again, he just moved over, making space for Sammy.

"It's a stray puppy," Charles jumped in to explain. "He turned up at David's house last night when we were —" He stopped.

"During the rainstorm." Quickly, David finished Charles's sentence, as if he knew Charles didn't want to tell Sammy about the campout just then.

But Sammy didn't even seem to notice a thing. "Cool." Sammy examined the puppy. "He's messy, but cute. He looks just like that dog Benji, in the movies. What's his name?"

"We don't know." Charles had hardly even had a chance to wonder about that. "He wasn't wearing a collar when we found him. Dr. Gibson loaned us one. And she sewed up a cut on his foot, see?" He pointed to the purple-wrapped paw.

"Where'd he come from?" Sammy wanted to know everything.

"We don't know that, either." Charles opened the door of the crate and let the puppy out. "He's a stray. Hopefully we can find his people soon and get him home."

The puppy began to wander around the kitchen, sniffing here and there as he explored this new place.

I smell another dog. I wonder if he's friendly.

Charles's dad took his sandwich out to his workshop, and the boys sat down to eat their lunch while Charles told Sammy all about how they'd first seen the puppy, and how he had kept trying to get away from them, running up the muddy path alongside the stream.

"He sure is a stinky guy." Sammy held his nose. "P.U."

"He can't help it. Anyway, we were just about to give him a bath. Want to help?" Charles knew Sammy would want to be in on the action. "I'll go run some water in the tub. Maybe you guys could get a plastic bag over his foot." Charles rummaged in a kitchen drawer to find a plastic bag and a big rubber band, which he handed over to David. Then he ran upstairs and turned on the taps in the bathtub. He made sure there were plenty of towels and got out the Bean's baby shampoo. Charles had learned a lot about giving baths to puppies. Lesson number one: Keep the door closed. Lesson number two: Don't use too much soap.

The tub had about two inches of water in

it when Sammy and David appeared in the bathroom. Sammy carried the puppy in his arms. The plastic bag covered the puppy's hurt foot. "Looks like you're all ready for us," said Sammy. He started to lower the puppy into the water.

NO! No, no, no, no, NO!

The little dog's legs pumped wildly as if he thought he could run away, even though Sammy was holding him tight.

"Wait." David stepped forward. "Go slowly. He's scared, can't you tell?"

Get me out of here!

The puppy's legs churned harder. Charles could tell how frightened he was. "David's right." Charles thought it was typical for Sammy to take over and start doing things without thinking.

"Let David do it. The puppy is starting to trust him."

Sammy shrugged and handed the puppy over to David. "Fine. You try."

David nuzzled the puppy's dirty neck. "How about a bath? It'll feel good." He spoke so softly that Charles could barely hear him. Then, slowly, he began to lower the puppy into the water. His legs began to churn wildly again.

No! Please, please don't make me go in the water.

"Boy." David stepped back from the tub and the puppy relaxed right away, licking David's cheek as if to thank him. "He really, really does not want a bath. He's shaking all over again. It's like he's terrified, like he's scared of *water*. Which is weird, since he always . . ." Suddenly, David's eyes lit up as if he'd had a brainstorm.

"Since he always heads right up the stream whenever he has the chance." Sammy finished the sentence. He nodded and smiled at David.

"So?" Charles didn't get the point.

"Think about it. First of all, why would the puppy be so, so afraid of water? And second, if he's so scared of it, why would he keep going up the stream?" Sammy acted as though the answers were obvious.

Charles shrugged. "Who knows?"

Sammy and David looked at each other. "We do." David sounded excited. "At least, we *think* we do!"

CHAPTER NINE

Charles still had no idea what his friends were talking about. He looked from one to the other, bewildered. "Do you guys mind telling me what you're talking about?"

"Let's get out of the bathroom first." David held the puppy firmly, close to his chest. "He's still really scared. No way are we going to get this puppy in that tub, at least not today."

Charles was surprised. David didn't seem so shy when he was standing up for the puppy. "Sure, let's go downstairs." He led the way back to the kitchen.

David put the puppy back into his crate and watched him curl up into the old towels.

David smiled down at the puppy. "I think he feels safe in there."

"So?" Charles put his hands on his hips. "Explain."

"It's like this." Sammy started right in. "The puppy is scared of water, right?"

"Really scared," David added.

"But he always goes back to the stream." Sammy paced around the kitchen, excited.

"And he always heads the same way. Upstream." Now David started pacing, too. The puppy watched as the two boys walked up and down. "Why?"

"That's what I'm asking." Charles rolled his eyes. "Why?"

"Because . . ." Sammy began.

"Because he *came* from upstream." David blurted it out. "He must have gotten washed away from his home during all the flooding last week. Can you imagine how scary that would be for a little puppy, to be swept away down the stream? He'd never want to go near water again."

Suddenly, Charles remembered something David's father had said about thinking they might have gotten washed away that night when they were camping. He had been kidding, but maybe that really could have happened, if the stream were high enough. And it had recently been higher — that's why the banks were all muddy. That little stream could easily have grown big enough to wash a little puppy downstream. "I get it. I get it!" Charles couldn't believe he had been so dumb. It seemed obvious now.

"Now all we have to do is figure out which towns are upstream from here," David began.

"Right, like Johnstown, for one. And then we can start asking around to see if anyone lost a puppy," Sammy finished.

Charles stared at them. What had happened to shy David? Maybe it helped that Sammy didn't even seem to notice or care that David was shy in the first place. It seemed as if all Charles's worries were for nothing. Sammy probably wouldn't even care if he found out about the campout. Maybe now all three of them would be friends.

"Let's go to the library and check the newspapers from other towns." Sammy jumped to his feet.

Now it was Charles's turn to have an idea. "No, let's go to my mom's office! They have newspapers from the whole state there." When David and Sammy agreed, Charles asked his dad to look after the puppy, then the boys headed out.

Charles liked to visit his mom at the newspaper office. For one thing, there was always a box of doughnuts near the coffee machine. The chocolate ones were Charles's favorite. For another, there were chairs you could spin around on, and paper clips to make chains out of, and free pads of paper you could take home for art projects.

When the boys arrived, Charles's mom was on the phone. "And that was on Tuesday?" She nodded as she scribbled notes. "And you spoke to the police at that time?" Charles's mom sometimes wrote the newspaper's police blotter, which meant she had to research stories about fender benders in the middle of town, bikes that got stolen, and cats that got stuck up trees.

When she was done, Mom turned to Charles. "What's up?" She smiled at Sammy and David. "Where's the puppy?"

"He's at home with Dad." Charles started to explain what they had figured out, and why they were there at her office. By the time he got to "So, we were thinking maybe the puppy washed downstream from some other town," Mom was on her feet, looking at a big map on the wall.

She traced a finger in a big arc north of Littleton. "Could be Johnstown, or Townsend, or maybe even Sharon." Then she went to a big filing cabinet along another wall and started to pull out newspapers. She handed a thick stack to each boy and told them to take them over to the big conference table in the middle of the room. "These are last week's papers, from when the flooding was really bad. Some towns had a lot of damage: bridges out, cars swept away, houses flooded, stuff like that. Look for the local news section. Watch for —"

"Any articles about a missing puppy." Sammy finished her sentence as he began to skim through the papers she had given him.

The room was silent for a few minutes.

Then, "Here's one!" yelled Sammy. "Oh. Oops. No. That's about a goat that ran away. Never mind."

Again the rustling of papers was the only sound.

Then David jumped to his feet. "This has to be him. This is from the *Townsend News*." He read out loud, "Lucky, a six-month-old gray-and-white puppy who 'looks just like Benji,' according to Dr.

Mark Little, his owner, disappeared during last Monday's storm and has not been spotted since. Dr. Little and his family have posted flyers all over town and have notified the police, but so far no leads have surfaced. Anyone with information about Lucky is encouraged to call Dr. Little at 555-3456."

Almost before David finished reading, Charles was punching the numbers into the phone on his mom's desk. "Hello?" His heart pounded. "Is Dr. Little there? I think we've found his family's puppy."

The woman on the other end sounded kind of old and creaky. "Well," she said slowly, "no, he's not here. I'm the only one home right now, well, besides little Finn and Olive, that is. I've come to stay and help watch my grandkids while my son and daughter-in-law clean up after all that terrible flooding."

"Oh, well . . ." Charles tried to speak slowly and loudly in case the woman was hard of hearing.

"Maybe you would know if this puppy we found belongs to the doctor and his family?"

"Puppy? Oh, yes, I suppose that puppy has gone missing. I believe her name is Lucky. She's gray and white, and rather shaggy."

Charles's face fell. "I'm sorry. I guess it's not your puppy after all." He said good-bye, hung up, and turned to face his friends.

CHAPTER TEN

"I guess we have to start over." Charles hated to give his friends the bad news. "That was the grandmother. She's staying with the family to help out after the flood. They're missing a puppy — but it's a *girl* puppy." He headed back to his stack of newspapers, sighed, and started to turn the pages again.

An hour later, they had not found one other article about a missing puppy, even though they looked through newspapers from as far away as fifty miles. Sammy kicked disgustedly at the leg of the table. "I don't believe this, man."

"I don't, either." David frowned, deep in thought. "You know what I keep thinking? Some people never can get it straight whether your pet is a boy or a girl. Like my aunt? She always calls our cat, Slinky, a 'he,' even though she's a 'she.' She even had kittens once. Slinky, that is, not my aunt."

"Wait, you have a cat?" Charles stared at David.

David nodded. "She's really, really shy. She always hides when company comes over. That's why we couldn't take care of the puppy. She doesn't even let anybody but me pet her."

Somehow Charles wasn't surprised. Not about David's family having a shy cat, and not about the cat letting only David pet her. "What color is she?"

"She's a tortoiseshell. That's a really special kind of coloring. She's brown and black and cream and orange. She's pretty." David smiled proudly. "But that's not my point. My point is that my aunt always calls Slinky a 'he.'"

"So?" Sammy frowned. "Oh. I see what you're saying. You mean —"

"You mean maybe that grandmother I talked to thinks her grandkids' puppy is a girl, but he's really a boy." Charles understood right away. "Hmm . . . you think I should call again?"

"Maybe — couldn't we just bring the puppy up there?" David asked. "To Townsend. I mean, they'd need to see him to be sure, anyway, right?"

"Right." Charles's mom had been working at her desk, but she must have also been listening to the boys. Now she got up and came over to join them. "I think that's a great idea. I was going to take some clothes and kitchen things up that way, anyway, to donate to people who got flooded out of their houses." She had grabbed a phone book and now she flipped it open and traced a finger along one page. "Little, 659 Maple Street, Townsend. I know where Maple Street is. How about it? I'll drive you up."

David had been blushing ever since Charles's mom said his idea was great. "Really?"

"Really. Let's go get that puppy."

At home, Mom loaded some boxes and bags and the puppy's crate into the van. Behind her, Charles carried the puppy in his arms. "I wish we'd had a chance to give you a bath," he told the puppy. "I'm sure you look even cuter when you're all clean." He kissed the top of the puppy's head, still soft despite its matted fur. The puppy gave him a big lick on the cheek. "If you do belong to them, I bet they'll be glad to see you no matter how you look."

The puppy snuffled in Charles's ear.

Where are we going now?

Charles gave the puppy a hug, put him into the crate, and closed the door.

On the way to Townsend, Charles started to see signs of the recent flooding. "Wow, check it out!" He pointed to a bridge that had been broken in half by raging water. The stream it crossed was calm again now. Charles could hardly imagine how powerful its flow must have been to do such damage. "I wonder how those people get to their house now." A little red house on the other side of the stream looked as if it had been hit hard by the flood, too. Mud filled the yard, boards were ripped off the lower half of the house, and the garage next to it was tilted on its foundation.

The boys watched out the windows, exclaiming over washed-out roads, mud-covered cars strewn along a field, and huge trees that had been uprooted. "Man, flooding is no joke," Sammy said. "It's easy to see how a puppy could have been washed downstream, if a car could be."

As they entered Townsend, Mom told them to help watch for street signs. "Maple Street is right around here somewhere.... Ah! Here we go." She took a right turn and, a few blocks later, swung the van into the driveway of a big brick house.

They all piled out, and Charles went to the

back of the van to get the puppy. As soon as he opened the door, he saw that the puppy was on his feet. He wagged his feathery tail, his eyes were shiny, and his furry, floppy ears were all perked up.

"Hey, you look happy." Charles opened the door of the crate and scooped the puppy into his arms. "Does this place look familiar?" Maybe they had come to the right place.

Mom led the way to the front door, but before they were even halfway up the brick walkway, the door flew open and a little boy about the Bean's age ran out, followed by a bigger girl. "Lucky!" The boy flung his arms open.

"You came home!" shouted the girl. They ran toward the puppy in Charles's arms.

Charles turned to grin at David. "I guess you were right."

"Yes!" David pumped his fist. "The Slinky theory holds true."

A man and an older woman followed the boy out the door. They watched as the boy reached up to pat the puppy. The puppy wriggled out of Charles's arms, and soon he and the kids were rolling around on the grass. The puppy's tail wagged a mile a minute as the kids kissed and hugged him. They laughed out loud and the puppy barked happily.

I knew I would find you. I knew it. I knew it!

The man laughed, too. "Well, well, well, look who's home." He smiled at Charles and the others. "Hello, I'm Mark Little. This is my mother, and those are my children, Finn and Olive." He shook hands all around as Charles and his friends introduced themselves. "We've been so worried. Lucky disappeared during the flood. We've been looking and looking for him. My wife, Heather, has barely slept. It's been six long days, and I can see he's had some adventures. Where did he turn up?"

David and Charles took turns telling the whole story. Sammy jumped in now and then to add a comment. Dr. Little wasn't surprised to hear how frightened Lucky had been when they first found him. "He's always been shy with people he hasn't met. But if he gets to know you —" He beamed down at Finn and Olive, who were still hugging and kissing Lucky. "Once he realizes that he's safe with you, he'll be your pal forever."

Charles looked at David. Maybe that was part of the reason David had understood Lucky so well. David was exactly the same way. Once he got to know you, David was hardly shy at all.

The grandmother laughed as she watched Lucky and the kids tumble around together. "She's certainly looking scruffy, but we're glad she's back. She really is such a good puppy."

Charles almost burst out laughing.

Sammy gave David a high five.

"Mom! Lucky's a boy, remember?" Dr. Little gave his mother an exasperated look. "But you're right. *He* is a very good puppy." Then he smiled at the boys. "And he sure has lived up to his name. He was one extremely lucky dog to have met up with you kids. I can't thank you enough for rescuing him and finding out where he belongs. And Dr. Gibson sure did a great job fixing him up. I'll send her a check right away." He shook hands all around, one more time.

The boys patted Lucky and said good-bye. Lucky licked each of their faces in return. When they got into the van to leave, Charles's mom turned around in her seat to look at the boys. "Good job, you guys." She held up a fist, and they all reached out for a bump.

As they drove off, waving good-bye to Finn,

Olive, and Lucky, David poked his head out the window to look up at the sky. "Hey, no more rain! The sun is out." He turned back to grin at Sammy and Charles. "It's a perfect night for a campout, don't you think?"

PUPPY TIPS

The same things that are dangerous for people, like hurricanes, floods, tornadoes, and wild-fires, can be dangerous for pets, too. During Hurricane Katrina in New Orleans, many pets were separated from their owners. People worked very hard to take care of those animals and help find their families. In some cases, when families had lost their homes and could no longer care for a pet, other families adopted those cats and dogs.

Make sure you and your parents have a plan for emergencies, and don't forget to include a plan for making sure your pets are safe.

Dear Reader,

David's mom was right about being careful around dogs you don't know. It's always smart to have an adult help if you are trying to catch a stray dog.

Once a stray dog followed me home when Django and I were out for a walk. He was scruffy and thin, but he was wearing a collar with tags on it, so I was able to track down his owners. They lived over three miles away! I kept him safe in my fenced yard while I waited for them to pick him up. If he had not been wearing a collar, I would have called the police and the local animal shelter to report a stray.

Yours from the Puppy Place,
Ellen Miles

P.S. To see how Charles and Lizzie got their start fostering puppies, read GOLDIE.

ABOUT THE AUTHOR

Ellen Miles likes to write about the different personalities of dogs. She is the author of more than 28 books, including the Puppy Place and Taylor-Made Tales series as well as *The Pied Piper* and other Scholastic Classics. Ellen loves to be outdoors every day, walking, biking, skiing, or swimming, depending on the season. She also loves to read, cook, explore her beautiful state, and hang out with friends and family. She lives in Vermont.

If you love animals, be sure to read all the adorable stories in the Puppy Place series!